D1058895

MARVEL
IRON MAN 3

IRON MAN FIGHTS BACK

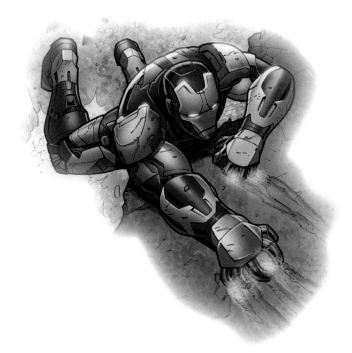

WRITTEN BY THOMAS MACRI

BASED ON A SCREENPLAY BY DREW PEARCE & SHANE BLACK

PRODUCED BY KEVIN FEIGE

DIRECTED BY SHANE BLACK

MARVEL
New York

marvelkids.com

TM & © 2013 MARVEL & SUBS.

Printed in the United States of America

First Edition

1 3 5 7 9 10 8 6 4 2

G658-7729-4-13032

ISBN 978-1-4231-7248-2

SUSTAINABLE
FORESTRY
INITIATIVE

Certified Chain of Custody
Promoting Sustainable Forestry

www.sfiprogram.org
SFI-01415

The SFI label applies to the text stock

This is Tony Stark.

Tony was having
a really bad day.

You see, Tony wasn't
feeling very well.

His girlfriend had become friends with someone he didn't like.

9

He had also been working too hard. Tony was trying to make the perfect Iron Man suit.

Sure, Tony was still Iron Man.

But he couldn't solve every problem.

His enemies hurt people.
They wound up in the hospital.
This made Tony angry.

Then the day got even worse.
His house was attacked!
It was the villain known
as the Mandarin.

Tony's house was being destroyed.
His friends had escaped.
But Tony stayed and fought back.
He put on his new Iron Man
armor and attacked!

But the Mandarin was smart.
His copters were really strong!
His house fell into the ocean.
Iron Man was trapped inside!

Tony had escaped in his Iron Man suit.
But his armor was damaged.
He flew as far away as he could.

The suit crashed into the snow.
It smoked and leaked oil.
It had stopped working.

Tony dragged his suit to an old shed.
Tony knew he had to fix his armor.
It was the only way to beat the villain.

Tony worked very hard.
He tried to fix his armor.
He worked all day.
He even worked all night.

Tony's hard work paid off.
He fixed it! Iron Man was back.
He was ready for a fight.

He flew up in the air.
He saved a lot of people.
He had made a bad day a little better.
Iron Man had fought back!